Slime Girl With Benefits

A Lesbian Monster Girl Erotica

Cithrel

Contents

1

Kindling

A handful of lanterns lit the underground library, just out of reach from potential kindling as light and shadow traded places across the amber space every so often. The air bore the scent of a dry forest, and the shuffling of paper echoed through the rows and rows of dusty shelves.

Janara's ears bobbed up and down while the noise intensified. When she rounded the corner, the sound peaked and her ears froze.

Another elf! She'd seen his kind tallied in the roster before, but they didn't update that thing very often, so the snow elf presumed them to be all gone.

There he was, sitting with his dusky face buried in an even duskier book. His hair was a tad darker than his skin, and his long ears dipped and rose with each breath. Dust elves were a rare sight since Mednessa's fall, but her kind wasn't a common sight in the desert, either.

Janara closed her eyes. Years of training had granted her a gracefully toned body—the standard for elven beauty. Was that not enough? Sure, she was a snow, and he was a dust, but they were both endangered elves and Coveners too.

She brushed her white hair back and held a breath as she walked into the line of fire of countless voices. It must have been a book club or something. Damn it, why did the table have to be so packed? Her past assignments involving bodyguarding, bounty hunting, and occasionally fishing didn't seem so bad now.

Her shoes tapped against the stone, louder than ever, and the figure across the dust elf pointed. Soon the entire table had set their sights on the elf, staring wordlessly as if they expected her to explain her appearance. Part of her wanted to peruse the nearest shelf and slink away.

Another part of her, however...

Janara's hands balled into fists, thankfully hidden by the robe's long sleeves. Her eyes shifted to the crackling lanterns on the walls, the pile of books on the table, and finally to that wonderful dust elf.

For a moment. Otherwise, it'd be weird if she didn't glance at the other Coveners as well.

"Wow, I didn't know we had another elf! Can I sit with you guys?" asked Janara.

The grinning snow elf's heart thumped like a drum as a chorus of yeses and yeahs greeted her. She scanned the table as she approached it. There were two empty spots, and one was next to him. Was it really this easy?

Janara's robe hid her quaking legs as they lifted over the bench, and a creak sounded as she added her weight to it. The cramped seating did not get along with Coven clothing, but it was a small price to pay to get this close to another elf.

The other Coveners wore their hoods up, and darkness obscured their faces. The largest among them had a green tinge, whereas the others held various shades from bright to brown. A range of soft and gruff voices echoed about as they introduced their ranks, roles, and maybe their names.

Janara wouldn't know, as she spent that time sneaking glances at her elven neighbor. Despite the distance, she could feel his warmth on her face and hands. How much warmer would he feel up close?

A voice broke through, matching his lips, and she turned to face him. "...Alsindor, initiate in the summoning division. You?" His book dropped onto the table with a thump that straightened her back.

His lovely red eyes pierced into her pale blue ones, making her heart flutter. But what was there to be worried about? Her baggy robe absorbed the shivers, and the terrible lighting masked the obvious blush on her face, right? And maybe he was nervous too, but she couldn't see that for the same reasons.

The snow elf's ears perked up. "Janara, also summoning!" She was also several ranks above him, but she'd rather not disclose such things.

"Oh? You must be in the other one." Alsindor's short hair shifted as his head rested on his hand, and his curious smile nearly melted her. "What's your familiar?"

Of course the Coven's only other elf would make it as hard as possible for her. "Eryss. She's a slime." Or a water elemental if one wanted to sound smart. At this rate, she was going to turn into water too. Sweat tickled her neck as she fidgeted with one of her long ears.

Alsindor did the same, rolling one of his eartips between his fingers as he frowned and looked around the room. "You... don't keep her around?"

A gruff yet feminine voice came from across the table, probably from that orcess. "Dude, who keeps a water familiar up in the desert?"

"Hey!" Alsindor gestured across the table. "I do demons, not slimes, okay?" His frown turned into a cute pout as he crossed and slammed his arms on the table.

"C'mon, I'm not even in summoning and I know that!" said an unfamiliar voice.

The first voice laughed. "More like *dusty* elf!" More laughter joined in and their fists almost collapsed the table. "You sure you weren't a diversity hire?"

Another voice joined in. "How many bit-the-dusts are even left, anyway?"

"Vultures..." Alsindor sighed before planting his frowning face into his hand. His fingers grasped his temples as he shook his head.

Janara's jaw slacked and her throat tensed, but no yelling came. Her pupils jumped between the hooded figures and the dust elf as she put a hand on her chest.

Her eyes and heart relaxed, and she drew in a cool breath. It might've been a troublesome, embarrassing event for the dust elf, but it was also an opportunity.

"Alsindor, I'd be happy to teach you everything about water elementals," Janara whispered into his ear. Her breath steadied as her hand slipped toward his shoulder, and her lips curled with hope. "Are you free—"

At that moment, a shelf-sized silhouette broke out from the corner of her vision, and the resulting wind messed Janara's hair. Footsteps cracked against the cobblestone floor as she turned her head toward the noise. A billowing black robe kept the creature's build unknown, and it tucked a massive book under its arm.

"Did you jesters forget this is a fucking library?" A female voice boomed from behind the two elves, and the table legs rattled against the floor. "Leave or shut up."

The voice was unmistakably demonic, and an unfittingly pink ribbon decorated one of her horns.

Her amber eyes cut through the dusk, scanning the group and eventually landing on the elves. Then they landed on Janara. Her slitted pupils and frown trembled while the snow elf withdrew her hand from Alsindor's shoulder.

The succubus seemed slightly happier after that.

"You're in my spot." Her hoof clicked against the floor as her hulking tail waved back and forth from behind.

Janara's eyes met hers as the snow elf pointed across the table. "There's an open seat over there."

A snap of the demoness's fingers dissolved the book she carried into nothingness, and her arms crossed under her chest. The demon's violet hands shook as she glared at the snow elf with narrowed eyes.

Janara glanced down at her own body for a moment before snapping back up with a blank expression.

Alsindor was firm as he rose and stood between the two, forcing the towering succubus back a step. "Lucretia's a bit... stubborn." It looked as if she wanted to strangle him as well. "Demon familiars, I know, right?" He weakly chuckled as his eyes darted between the two.

Was it something in the air?

The snow elf's eyes couldn't help but wander to Lucretia's form again. Their robes were more or less identical, but the demon's had little slack compared to hers. A thorough inspection of the succubus's chest and waist explained everything.

Janara ran her hand across her own torso. Beautiful as elves were, their bodies tended to be petite, and she was no exception, being both slender and athletic. Other species had more dimorphic bodies, and plenty passed Janara on her way to the library. She had given their physiques little thought.

So why was she thinking about this succubus differently? The snow elf shook her head. Succubi looked like that by design to steal mortal souls. It'd be an insult to her dignity to surrender her gaze and thoughts to one. Besides, they specialized in targeting men, right? So why did she feel so—

"My eyes are up here." Lucretia's voice made the elves jump.

Someone else... It had to have been one of those idiots in the back... Not her, no way...

A snicker from behind ambushed Janara, and her vision bounced back up as a rumble traveled through her spine.

Blessed were the library's terrible lanterns and the Coven's amazing robe for hiding things so well. Her thighs felt heated as she squeezed them together, and her cheeks glowed brilliantly. Whose idea was it to build a library underground, anyway? What a terribly sticky, hot, and musky place to put one.

"Alsindor." Lucretia wickedly grinned at the dust elf before pointing a finger at Janara. "Tell your boyfriend to stop staring at my chest."

Janara blinked.

More snickers cracked behind the snow elf, and her face tensed as she grit her teeth. The two elves shared rosy faces now, all for the wrong reasons. Janara widened her eyes and mouth and threw her arms into the air. "Excuse me? I'm very much a woman!"

"Are you sure about that? The evidence falls... *flat*." Lucretia put her hand to her mouth, giggling as her chest bounced and swayed. With premeditation.

That broke the floodgates.

Terrible, terrible sounds crashed through the library. Even with her palms flattening her ears and her fingers in the holes, it was all Janara could hear.

Alsindor ran his mouth at Lucretia as he shook the succubus back and forth—or at least tried to, given how she was several heads taller than him. As for his words, the chaos and her hands drowned out whatever he was saying. Not that Janara had any curiosity left.

Shelf after shelf flashed before the snow elf's eyes as she stumbled into a sprint.

The exit... Where was it...?!

2

Refuge

Shimmer Canyon.

To some, its towering cliffs and carcasses served as warnings, but to others, they were landmarks on a path home. A path to one of the last havens for monsterkind.

Only monsterkind. Death was the only destiny that manifested here for those unwelcome. Too bad for the humans, but they had enough places to live, honestly. Couldn't they leave this one place alone?

Long was the trip back to town, and the grainy winds sharpened by the minute. The sand tinted her once white garb and stung her skin. Even for an elf of snow, it was an all too familiar sensation.

Her yearnings for the northern tundras and mountains had dulled over time. This was her home, now and forever, and the joys and pains of desert life were just that—part of life itself. It was a simple choice, given the alternative.

Maybe one day she could go back. Back to the glowing, ribboned skies that stretched for miles. Back to the pale mountains and tundras with slumbering chills that desert nights could only tease. Devouring roasted sculpin and cloudberry-topped shaved ice...

But that day was not today.

She reached the same jagged boulder that greeted her at the start of every return trip. Crawling between the rock and the cliff wall brought her to the entrance of a cave. Her footsteps grew wetter as the rough sands transitioned to a soft mossy carpet, and the winds dulled to a murmur.

She had used this dainty hideaway many times before for weathering the weather, and it had never lost its luster.

Droplets echoed along the rusted walls, water trickled in and out of the porous pools, and a waterfall was heard but not seen. Rays beamed down from the ceiling's cracks and refracted off the mist into vibrant hues.

The air was chilly, reminding her of a long forgotten place as she approached the largest pool in the center. The light was strongest there, and a pair of soothing eyes stared back at her from the basin, breaking with the occasional ripple.

What a perfect place to relax.

"Aaaargh!"

The reflection turned ugly and the snow elf whipped her desert garb into a glistening wall behind her with a loud crack. Grains of sand littered the air, and her panting made her cough and sputter, overtaking the cave's song.

Stupid, stupid! What a waste of time. Trying to court him with a full table?! What was she thinking? Gods, that was pathetic. Humiliated in front of all those people. Humiliated in front of that cute elf. All she had to do was wait. Wait for when he was alone, without that demon bitch around, and then make her move.

She was so aggressive, too. Were they fucking? They were definitely fucking. It was a truth that succubi enjoyed laying with their summoners the most, and an unspoken one that it was not entirely one-sided.

How typical that he'd choose flimsy pleasures over the consummate. Path of least resistance and all that. It was all about the exterior, and as graceful as Janara was, her mortal figure just couldn't compete with the supernatural.

The elf sighed as she rubbed her temples. A dip in the pools, a pleasant chat with Eryss, a nap, and then another chance would grace her... eventually.

As her mind started plotting, she squatted next to the pool and extended her hand while focusing on her palm. A wrinkled gray orb gathered into existence, and she gently lowered it in. Water swirled around the desiccated heart before the liquid bubbled, thickened, and rose.

Eryss's core.

It centered itself within the growing sea-green pile as her head and torso formed. Then came her arms and half of her thighs before the water covered the rest. Underwater, Eryss's legs converged into a layered pile that made up her solitary 'foot'. Rippling parts of it in sequence glided her across the ground, sort of like how a snail or slug moved.

Regardless of the original water's properties, she always smelled like a crisp lakeside breeze, to her summoner's delight.

Slimes, snow elves, and deserts. Janara chuckled while a face formed in the watery clump. She sat on her haunches a safe distance away, not wanting to be splashed just yet.

A single mass defined Eryss's hair, running down her back with some parts fused to it and some not. It was a richer blue-green color that reminded Janara of seaweed. The free strands splattered against the slime's glassy membrane every so often.

Beneath her skin, her fluids gushed between her head and torso, bobbing her magenta nucleus up and down in a relaxing rhythm. Vivid fragments danced along the walls as Eryss passed under a faint sunbeam.

The elemental looked so statuesque in the middle of the pool.

With a body that could take on any shape, and an endless amount of material, Eryss was resourceful. Her featureless breasts jiggled and dripped with the subtlety of an ocean, while her waist, hips, and belly remained defined against an otherwise animated backdrop. Runny globs littered her membrane, but it did little to reduce a figure that would've made even a succubus blush.

Not Janara, though. Nope. Lucretia might have made her feel funny with her big... personality, but Eryss was a pure being, who was only to be gazed at for meditation. And appreciation, like an elaborate fountain. That's why the elf never asked her to tone it down.

Nothing wrong with admiring excellence, right? Even if it was another woman's body. Beauty was power and Eryss just looked so powerful.

"Janara?" The slime's raspy voice prickled the elf's ears.

"Sorry, there's been a lot on my mind today." The elf exhaled as her slime nodded.

Janara blinked and shook her head before staring into the elemental's eyes. Unlike the rest of her sea-green body, her eyes—irises and all—shared her nucleus's color. The violet pigments within each pupilless organ swirled around like miniature whirlpools.

"Umm..."

The elf smirked at her. "Don't worry, I'll tell you all about it."

Eryss's face lit up as she flowed toward the rocky edge of the pool. Her arms rested against it as her lower half churned the water.

A shiver ran down the snow elf's spine as she rose, and perspiration rushed down her leg into the vegetation. Her toes scrunched the moss underneath, drawing out moisture as if it were a rag.

Maybe her woes worsened the desert heat. Her bra was damp and her underwear dripped with sweat as she flung both into her dusty pile of outerwear.

Nothing covered her now, but the elf bore no blushes—they had bathed together countless times before, and in this same pool, too.

Janara's foot dipped into the water before the rest of her splashed in. As her pulse fell and her skin's dust washed away, a heated breath left her lips. It was no doubt freezing for anyone who wasn't a snow elf or slime, and that thought gave her a bit of joy while the chill swaddled her.

The slime floated closer, bringing along slightly warmer waters that loosened the elf's muscles. With her sore back and elbows resting on the pool's mossy rim, Janara closed her eyes and cleared her throat.

"Where to start..." said the elf.

3

Ichor and Shame

Stalactites dripped and dropped, currents shushed and gushed, and the sandstorm outside whispered and cracked as the last echo of the snow elf's tale faded into the earth.

Janara sunk into the water until just her eyes peeked out from the surface. As usual, she had told her friend everything, and the water gave her burning face some relief.

The slime's nucleus danced from side to side as if it were searching her soul for an answer. "He clearly likes you. Whether that's friendship or something more, I'm not sure."

Only Janara's chin touched the water now. Her eyes fretted while the events in the library replayed in her mind. That cute smile and the small talk they had... It wasn't like he was distant to the snow elf or anything. He probably would've loved to learn more about water elementals with her, and he didn't laugh or look too pleased with his succubus's wordplay.

"Maybe..." said Janara.

Damn those other Coveners, though. Filthy vultures. Greeting her like that, only to turn on her at the first sign of blood. Their faces, clothes, and voices were unworthy of her memories. What did they know about elves, anyway?

Since the Coven operated outside of the law, it was no surprise that such individuals were part of its ranks.

She nearly smiled, but then the memories raced through her again. Eryss was a large part of her life, and Lucretia probably played a similar role for Alsindor beyond the presumed superficialities. So it was with reasonable summoners and familiars.

"If only I met Lucretia differently." That succubus had to have known of the elven plight and of Janara's intentions from the start. Still, she went for the snow elf's throat. "Was it the seat?"

"Possibly a case of jealousy." A few droplets fell from the slime's chin as she spoke. "You *are* threatening to take her favorite food away. What would she do if you two got together?"

"Eat to her heart's content?" Janara twisted her ear between her fingers. "I'd be willing to share, somewhat. But I couldn't really explain that to her in front of everyone."

"A private meeting ought to give you the peace you need." Eryss dabbled with her glob of hair, dispersing plenty of ooze into the water. "Why don't you follow them home next time?"

"And if they don't appreciate being stalked?"

"I doubt he'll mind. As for his succubus..." Eryss's eyes glowed as the surrounding water thickened for a moment. "I'd love to return the favor."

"Really? You're the best!" Goo splattered everywhere as the elf hugged Eryss. The syrup running down Janara's back was faintly warm, as was the slime's membrane squished against the elf's chest.

"It's the least I can do for my best friend." The slime hugged her in return, smothering the elf with her form. "That lake was really, really cold." Eryss shivered.

It'd be a while before they'd be called to the hideout again, but just the hope soothed the tragedy. Some of it. In Janara's head, the events splintered into countless time-lines. What if she did this? What if she did that? Would it have played out the same?

"Ow!" A wince severed the elf's thoughts as the slime's hands ran over a few purplish spots on her back.

Eryss's body swelled as she spoke and bubbles popped atop her head. "Bruises! Did Lucretia—?!"

"Clumsy me fell a few times during training." Janara chuckled and turned her back to the slime. "See?"

"I could have spotted for you. Selfless elf." Eryss sighed as she pressed her gooey chest against her back. "Hang on, this will sting a little."

They'd hugged before, but it felt so different this time around. Sure, it was all goo, and she didn't mean it that way, but Janara still shivered as the slime's breasts coated her back in gentle heat.

Was Lucretia just as big under her robe...?

The living liquid flowed through the elf's gaps to her front, and the slime's heartbeat prodded everything in between. Some parts more than others, and Janara's pulse raced as her jaw clenched.

Fingers and magic were pittances compared to this. Good thing they weren't facing each other, for blood stirred in her face.

And elsewhere.

The goo rushed over something far more delicate as it coated every part of her inner thighs, and her mind

couldn't help but concentrate on that part of her. Its hairlessness left it at the mercy of Eryss's vibrations. Every tremor gathered a familiar sensation from within, and it seeped out of her.

It soared higher and higher, and the elf's muscles and nipples firmed as electricity arced through her ears. The world spun around her as her breath threatened to burn a hole through her hand.

"Aieeeeee!" Janara's squeak pierced her teeth and palm before it wandered through the cave.

The elf's athletic thighs wrung the water from the mass between her legs, only for her elven fluids to quench it once more like an obscene water cycle. The slime offered just enough resistance to stop the elf from slipping underwater.

Eryss liquified for a moment before she climbed and clung to the elf's body again. "Hey, I haven't even started yet! Surely giving that dustie a good view on all fours is worth a little pain."

"I'm... ready now." Janara wasn't, and her slime's quip didn't help.

How much did Janara spill into Eryss, and how did the elemental not notice? She closed her eyes, swallowed a knot of drool, and steadied her breath.

Slime flattened against the crease in the elf's back as Eryss drilled thousands of tiny watery blades into her skin. A sharp pain followed her stray blood on the way out, yet it felt rather nice, like a humble acupuncture session.

The cuts on the elf's skin shut as Eryss bonded flesh and slime, bringing forth a tingling sensation. Then her body was spotless, and it was all over.

Eryss flicked one of the elf's ears, making her flinch. "Told you it wouldn't be that bad."

"Yeah..." With the surgery concluded, the gel binding Janara thinned, and she submerged herself again, peeling off Eryss before slipping away. The elf resurfaced with her back to the edge of the pool.

She ran a hand across her trembling chest and face, sighing from the lukewarm feeling before smiling at Eryss. "Fully relieved!"

Her shout subsided with the pool's waves, and the native song of the cave returned. The air remained guilty with the unforgettable tinge of a lonely night, but only for those who noticed such minor things.

"I'd imagine. Coming after a rough day is quite relieving, wouldn't you say?" The elemental smirked.

Those like Eryss.

The elf's face stained with blood once more while her back straightened against the padded rock. "You were rubbing against me a lot, okay? And I was... congested."

"I can tell. Usually, you taste much milder!" Ichor and shame swirled and bubbled within Eryss for a moment before dissolving throughout her translucent body with a fizzle. "Ahh, delicious."

Janara had watched Eryss digest plenty of rations before, but seeing her elven fluids become part of the slime's body confused her loins.

The slime submerged, and the pool rumbled as she spoke through it. "You were ogling my body back then, as well. Did that succubus awaken something in you?"

Those like Eryss!

"Of course not! You're just very... soothing to stare at. Like a river. Besides, can't I admire a fellow woman's physique?" The elf pouted as she gazed into the water and tugged an ear.

The water formed into a familiar face before the slime rose over the elf. The two were closer than ever now, and Janara could feel the heat emanating from Eryss. Or was it her own being reflected?

"I can taste it in your fluids." Eryss put her hand in the middle of the elf's shivering chest, making her jump. "Look at you, just my touch can make you melt." The slime giggled as her hands engulfed the elf's.

Janara's eyes widened as they immersed themselves in the slime's gaze.

"I wouldn't mind doing it with such a cute and tasty elf like you." Eryss smiled. "Don't give me that look. If Dusty can have his succubus, why can't you have me?"

Janara blinked and swallowed.

"Erm! You and I are..." Janara's voice pinched to a whisper, and the elf wrung the slime's hands. "We're both umm, you know...?"

"Sexy monsters in need of relief. You like my body, and I like yours. Isn't that all that matters?" Eryss leaned closer, splattering her breasts over the elf's tight chest. "Besides, don't you want to learn how to win Lucretia's favor?"

A tingle tormented the edge of her nethers.

Small bubbles emanated from within Eryss, traveling to and popping on all her surfaces as the air thickened with an aquatic aura. The teasing scent clung to Janara's lungs and mind, replacing part of her worries with something else.

Eryss looked more inviting than ever. Gods, what an indulgent body she had shaped for herself. Tuned like a succubus, and maybe even beyond that. Its equivalent in flesh would have magnetized the eyes of every man and woman in Stygia. Yet here the slime was, pressed up against her.

Her! A dainty elf often mistaken for a man from afar. Fawned over by such a potent being whose curves made her definitively ladylike at any distance.

Alsindor was probably hatefucking Lucretia *right* now. Screaming at her. Berating her. All while filling a cradle unworthy of endangered seed. Multiple times, probably. Calming and gorging himself on merciless pleasures that only a supernatural being could give.

So why was Janara so reluctant to do the same? Was she scared she'd ruin her chances with him if he found out? A depraved dust elf would've found a depraved snow elf more alluring, not less. They could exchange lewd tales with ankles over shoulders and chests to chests...

...with their familiars watching, or even... taking part.

It was only fair for the elf to indulge in her familiar as well. No, not fair. Necessary. The scuffle in the library left her just as denied and on edge, and she needed to be calmed and gorged, too. Grinding on the slime softened her, but now she needed to be thawed.

Janara sighed as she stared at their connected chests. Goo drowned her silken skin all the way down, squeezing and pulling every inch of her as she dripped into Eryss's body.

A mere scratch of the surface did all that. Yet they hadn't even begun. Her mind whirled at the possibilities, and at last, her voice caught up to her feelings.

"You're right, it doesn't matter."

4

Shy Snow

One day, Eryss would tell Janara of her past life as a human, but until then, the snow elf could only wonder how she was so skilled.

A few paces from the pool atop the soaked moss, Janara laid on her back with her legs spread. The elf had been naked in front of Eryss before, but she had never been this... accessible.

Their fronts sandwiched together as sweat and slime alike mixed in the seams, and their lower halves diverged as Eryss's stretched into the half-emptied pool. There, her membrane pulsed as it drew in water.

"You're so cute when you're embarrassed." As her syrupy hand played with Janara's ear, Eryss resumed licking at the elf's neck.

Schlick, schlick. The noise shivered her as each lap left a balmy residue across her skin that remained animated long after being detached from the slime. It teased the elf between Eryss's licks, and Janara fought off the urge to laugh.

Heaps of goo pulled on the elf as gravity spread Eryss upon her, making it hard to move. Not that she wanted to. She was like a living blanket of sorts, and if Janara had any less willpower, its weight and undulations could've lulled her to a very pleasured sleep.

A rough lick from the elemental forced a moan from Janara, and her hand skimmed the surface of the slime's head. Janara's fingers squeaked against her membrane as her other hand held onto its gooey counterpart at their side. Every pleasured bliss traveled to the slime as a squeeze, and she felt more connected to her than ever.

Another moan and Eryss went lower. Her tongue traced its way down to a faint bump before it ascended to its apex. As Eryss latched onto the pink nub, alternating between sucking and licking, it hardened and Janara nearly crushed the slime's hand in her grip.

Warmth nestled deep into her breasts from each intensifying suckle, which would've overwhelmed Janara had the slime not relieved her with those circling licks.

The same sensation repeated on the elf's opposite nipple. Eryss's hand had suctioned tight to her other breast, and through the translucency Janara could see something that mimicked a mouth. It wasn't a surprise that Eryss could do that with her body, but the thought that she'd go to such lengths for her was... Slimes were certainly something, alright.

Being serviced by two mouths at the same time was also interesting. It felt both pure and depraved at the same time. Pure in that it was her best friend doing it to her, and depraved in that she experienced a pleasure that usually required three participants. It was a duality that only a slime could've blessed her with.

Her nethers dampened within the pile of goo that swamped her loins.

The slime's head and hand pulled away, stretching the elf's breasts into small tents as her moans turned into cries. But they could only stretch so much, and a pop eventually broke their union. Two red marks prickled with bliss on the elf's pale chest as Eryss crept lower.

Her tongue dabbed the elf's belly button a few times before crossing the last crease of her faint abs. The living residue prodded her navel as her tongue dragged over the elf's mound, and Janara couldn't help but giggle.

Only peach fuzz guarded her sex, so when the slime planted a sloppy kiss there, the sensation traveled deep into the elf's flesh, turning into a shiver.

The elemental pecked lower, hitting a special spot, and the feeling radiated through the elf's groin. Janara squirmed as a heated trickle ran down to her rear.

"Can I?" Eryss's tongue ran across her gooey lips.

Janara looked at her own body. A shiny blue-green trail painted her body from her ears to her groin. As if it had a mind of its own, it stroked and squeezed her skin, even as Eryss's focus was elsewhere. Despite how thin the coating was, it still felt heavy.

And there Eryss was, snuggled between her legs and close enough for Janara to feel the chill of her membrane. Soon she would become even more acquainted with it. Everything seemed so meticulously practiced, as if Eryss had been waiting for Janara to open up to her this whole time.

That was a conversation for a different time, so Janara nodded.

The frosted organ made its maiden lick from the base of the elf's slit to the hardening nub on top, draining the me that had gathered within her folds. As her hips shivered and humped against the slime in response, the elf's hands scrunched the sticky moss at her sides.

Another lick went deeper, revealing the tongue's animated surface. When her tongue rested against the elf's entrance, Janara felt the membrane whirling across her clit, and her body rewarded Eryss with an adorable moan and another helping of juices.

Globules of elven essence drifted from the slime's head into her torso before being absorbed into her core, and Janara couldn't help but watch as her fluids joined the slime's form and scent. The slime's body darkened and warmed. And from Eryss's expression, she definitely enjoyed the act as well.

The elf swallowed and tapped on the slime's head.

Yeeeeessss...? Eryss's voice slithered into her mind.

Janara goofily smiled at her. "Can you, umm... go deeper?"

The slime giggled before squashing her cheeks into Janara's inner thighs. Her tongue splattered against the elf's entrance before reforming. After a bit more pressure, the elf's tightness surrendered, and her membrane seeped inside. Janara's abs flexed as she loosed a breath.

This time, Eryss rested her tongue within the elf. Her heartbeat drummed through her form, matching Janara's as the goo pulsed and swirled against the elf's walls. It churned as the slime's organ ballooned within her.

When Janara's hole buckled against her expanding presence, the tongue twisted in and out of her. Its size couldn't be any more perfect—large enough to grind against her special spots, yet forgiving enough for her inexperienced insides. Her abdomen clenched repeatedly and her waist bucked against the slime's efforts.

The elf rested her head on the vegetation and immersed herself in the cave's ceiling, trying to make sense of things.

To boil Eryss's existence down to her femininity would have been pure ignorance. She was a best friend, irreplaceable partner, and perfect confidant who understood, appreciated, and cared for Janara so much. That was what made this perfect. And by coincidence, she just so happened to be another woman.

Of course, that nuance wasn't to be completely disregarded. Eryss certainly knew the ins and outs of her body more than any man would have. She had kissed, licked, and prodded all the right places with no instructions or awkward reminders and she had done so with unbelievable patience. There was no rush, no pressure, and no mismatch in desires.

A spiking pleasure in her clit carried her out of her thoughts. It was something thin from the slime, like a finger or tendril, and it penetrated deep into her nerves as it pumped her nub from root to tip. Despite its size, it shared the same energy as Eryss's tongue and it soon brought her to the melting point.

The tongue's texture turned grainy, and each of its thrusts shivered her waist and forced out so much of her juices that some had to leak out unabsorbed.

Gods, no one had ever done this to her before, and her heat was about to tip over and spill. Was Janara supposed to give a warning or something?

A tingling sensation claimed the back of her head, and a raspy voice frothed in her mind. *Don't hold back... You deserve this...*

Plap, plap, plap... Janara closed her eyes and imagined the monstrosity inside her as its pounding pitched Janara's moans higher and higher. A familiar itch fumed through her ears and she held her breath as her hands wrung Eryss's goo out of the vegetation.

A final thrust surged against every vulnerability within her.

"Aaaaaagh!" Fever crested from her knife-ears, surging down her body in waves that strengthened with each throb. Her body rippled and writhed against Eryss, wringing her goo as the elemental fought to stay where she belonged.

Janara's hips plunged into the air, renewing the membrane's kiss against her sweetest parts until her hole collapsed. As her abs hollowed, her interior wrung the ooze within the juicy tongue, coating her insides and inner thighs in a brilliant glow that left her gasping and drooling.

Her back arched as her thighs squeezed together. Fluids crushed out of Eryss until the elf's legs cut her into two halves across the drenched floor. The slime rejoined soon after and gurgled as she blotted the elf's leftover fluids.

The rest of the slime withdrew from the now empty lake, joining the flood beneath the elf as her nucleus glided across Janara's chest. It pulsed as fast as the elf's heart and whereas her goo was warm, her core was boiling. Any hotter and it would've branded Janara's skin. For now, though, it was just a pleasing heat.

It always felt a bit lewd seeing how much bigger Eryss was in her humanoid form—breasts and all—but Janara never expected to feel the same about a giant puddle under her.

Goosebumps scattered across Janara's skin as the formless goo lifted the elf a few inches off the ground. When her hands held the fist-sized core to her chest, it seemed to beat even harder.

"You were amazing." Janara's first few breaths burned her lips. "Do slimes like being licked, too?"

The surrounding ooze vibrated until Eryss's voice was clear. "Can't say. I've never been licked before. Why?"

5

Shyer Water

Their positions were reversed from before, with Eryss's legs splayed out atop a viscous mass while Janara's head peeked out between her runny legs. As goo and flora cushioned her, the elf leaned closer to her membrane and inhaled the dizzying blend of elven and earthen scents.

Then she dug in.

Eryss rippled as the elf kissed her crotch, and although she was barren there, just their positions were enough to stir Janara's loins. She hooked her arms around the slime's smothering thighs and peered across her shiny belly, lively breasts, and, of course, her gorgeous face.

So this was what Eryss saw. Janara wasn't *that* nervous, was she? And there was no way her smile could have been that lovely.

The elemental had even molded herself a navel. Long gone were the days of snailing around as a blob and being called *it* by the Coveners and Stygians. Shamefully, Janara had done the same by accident a few times.

Her mastery of her amorphous form had shaped a body that must've reflected... no, *exceeded* her past life's allure.

Her tongue slithered across the slime's skin, and her lips drew in the surface's sheen. It held a hint of the sweet earthiness of the cave's spring and a very noticeable elven tang. She gave the taste a few swishes in her mouth before swallowing and skimming the slime's lukewarm membrane for more.

"I don't feel anything." Eryss frowned. "Yet another thing I miss..."

Oh, slimes. Literal bodies of water that lacked a nervous system. Great for combat, but not so great for the bedroom. Janara sighed. There had to be something she could do.

Hmmm...

It looked so tranquil as it swayed and pulsed inside her torso! When it was against the elf's chest, it felt unbelievably fleshy and soft.

Her lips curled, and a few seconds later, the slime caught her glance.

A tremor ran through Eryss's fluids, and her core shivered as the slime beneath foamed. "Absolutely not! I could barely endure your hands!" The nucleus fled to the top of her head, and her membrane stiffened, preventing any sort of access.

The ingested goo was like lava in her stomach as the cave spun around her. Powerful winds battered the cave from outside, and debris scattered into the other pools. In her current state, those sounds turned to mush in her ears. A shake of her head dispelled the curse for now.

"What did it feel like?" asked Janara.

"A stinging pain and a tinge of something else." While Eryss's hand clutched her chest, her skin alternated between being soft and hard, and her core fluttered in her head. "I... I don't know if we should..."

"My tongue's softer than my hands and I'll be extra gentle."

"What if it ends up... not being good?"

"We'll stop and I'll never ask again. How about that?"

Her heart stilled at the bottom of her head. "Also, I don't taste weird, do I?"

"You taste fine! Relax and let your bestie take care of you."

Eryss nodded as her nucleus descended back into her chest, right above her breasts.

Janara waded through her until their waists aligned, and then the elf flipped over. Now they were both on their backs, nearly sharing the same space and position. Eryss, having sucked up a miniature lake, enveloped the elf in her body. Thankfully, some selective thickening and shifting brought the elf into a comfortable pose within her.

The nook of the slime's neck hugged the back of her head perfectly as her ears skimmed its sides. The elf stretched her limbs and her legs floated within Eryss's foot. She kicked at the ticklish fluid there a few times, stirring up bubbles before she relaxed against the goo.

It was cozy being snuggled up against Eryss like this, way cozier than her actual bed, and the view was unmatched as well. With their chests layered on top of each other, it almost looked like Janara was the endowed one.

And the way those mounds swayed from her subtle movements as if they were actually hers! Janara had never felt so alluring before. There was a certain weight and momentum to them that just felt so natural and so... tingly. She was dripping down there again, wasn't she?

The slime's breasts overflowed her hands as she jiggled them up and down a few times before giving them a squeeze. The pressure rippled through the goo and onto her own breasts, and she felt her touch with a slight delay. While Janara's chest wiggled from the alien sensation, the ooze swirled around her nipples, making her shudder and clench her teeth.

There were so many possibilities, but as much as she wanted to drift off or explore their combined bodies, it'd be wrong to leave Eryss unsatisfied right now, especially after all the work the slime had put into the elf's joy.

Janara fished for Eryss's core, which playfully dodged her fingers as she swept them across her chest for it. Nothing could escape the devoted elf for long, and she eventually scooped it into her hands.

She rotated the nucleus in her grip, shuffling her fingers across its otherworldly texture and weight. Its dormant state had the surface of a dry rock, but now it was fleshy like the inside of her cheeks. Deep grooves littered its surface, and it beat like a heart as she closed her fingers around most of it.

The elf dragged the core around their mingling fronts, rubbing its foreign texture across her torso and belly and leaving shivers and bumps in its wake. Plenty of fluid leaked from the heart, and its warmth swaddled her faint breasts and abs.

Janara circled the organ around her nipple until it firmed, and she trembled as her nub flicked across the nucleus's creases. Eryss gurgled in return, and the core's ridges pinched her breast as the surrounding slime turned choppy. It initially stung and Janara gasped, but she soon moaned as the pain became bliss.

Hmmm, what to do next... Janara closed her eyes as her curiosities converged into a plan.

It took some effort to peel the core off her chest, and it finally did so with a pop. After her tongue drenched her lips, Janara brought the heart to her mouth, and a watery murmur sounded behind the elf as she raised the slime's violet orb to her pale blue eyes.

While most of the core's clinging slime had unraveled on its ascent, one tendril remained, linking the organ to the lumpy film edging her neck. It held an elastic resistance that refused to break.

The nucleus felt much heavier, and her fingers could only surround it halfway now. Did it swell from all her teasing? It certainly smelled stronger now.

Would it taste stronger, too?

When she pressed her wet lips to Eryss's core, bubbles rose from the bottom of the slime, tickling her inner thighs and armpits. The elf would've thrashed about, but the goo also thickened around her body, freezing her in that pose and leaving her defenseless against them.

After her laughter and struggles ceased, Janara tapped her tongue against a crease on the pulsating organ, and the slime's body liquified as an uncharacteristic cry came from Eryss, resembling a sound she'd make while in pain. Her fluids congealed over a few seconds and she reformed around the elf.

Janara retreated her tongue and stared into the nucleus. "Are you hurt? Do you want me to stop?"

"No... It's been so long since I've felt like this." The slime hugged the elf from behind, and her arms fused to the slick on her chest and neck. "Don't stop. It feels... good."

A deeper lick vibrated the core as her tongue dragged across its surface, and the slime rained goo everywhere. The secretions glued her tongue to the core, and Janara grew sore quickly, but she pressed on. While Eryss's insides fluttered around the elf, the liquid outside her membrane splashed. The turbulence teased Janara's nethers, and their grunts matched as she shivered and dripped into the water elemental.

The once calm Eryss softened, and the result streamed across the unimmersed parts of the elf's body. The living trails tickled goosebumps out of her as they wiggled like tiny snakes.

Naughtiness inflamed Janara as the slime tightened with every lick she made. Soon, Janara would give Eryss her first orgasm as a slime. How would it feel to be inside her at that moment?

Those two filthy thoughts raced the elf's heart.

One hand held the core to her mouth as the other slid down to her elven mound. Her fingers stroked her hardening nub in tandem with her licks and Eryss's contractions. Eventually, the slime ebbed and flowed between her legs, lathering her entrance in sticky fluid while her fingers smeared it over her clit. The goo traveled deep into her fleshy hood, and the elf's toes curled as it reflected Eryss's motions.

Her fingers had never moved so fast before, and soon her pussy clenched over and over. The rush of goo in and out of her folds fluttered her ears as each intake was warmer and thicker than the last.

Eryss's motions, but not her voice, diminished with every lick until her liquid stilled. Janara crammed her tongue between the nucleus's folds as her hand brought it closer to her mouth, hitting deeper and deeper spots.

Janara recalled the slime's work on her nethers and twisted her tongue in the narrow space, spreading Eryss's essence throughout her taste buds. Fluid resembling the elf's own juices spilled out of the core, and the further she delved, the muskier and tighter it became, until the tip of her tongue raked against something coarse.

"Aaaaahng..." The elemental's wail tingled her ears while it reverberated within her membrane.

The core's squeezes and emissions intensified as the elf and slime's flesh scraped against each other. Janara's mouth filled as fast as she could swallow until some had to overflow down her chin. Moments later, there was nothing—no more dripping, squeezing, or any sounds—and the slime froze.

One more lick and Eryss would've turned into water, but Janara had a better, filthier idea.

Her thoughts wandered through their shared comfort. The touch of her fingers was enjoyable, but rubbing them into her folds over several years had become routinely dull. Likewise, there was little fun to be had with toys that were too smooth or rough for her delicate yet demanding insides.

Eryss's core was different. It could soften or tighten by her will, and ravishing bumps adorned its surface. Janara's tongue and nipples had thoroughly enjoyed its texture, and soon another part of her would enjoy it.

The slimy spit connecting their organs together broke when she dragged the slime's core down her body. Her skin had absorbed some of the slick from before, enhancing its existing lusciousness. The goo stiffened her nipples, groped her abs, and clenched against her folds. As she rolled the core over her clit, its syrupy heat pounded into the nub with every pulse, and her jaw clenched.

Up and down, up and down. Their combined juices cheered Janara on as she ran the nucleus against her slit.

Ecstasy demanded more ecstasy, and the elf's hand blurred as a sloppy noise spoiled the ambiance. Lust churned within Janara, and her hips pushed back, doubling her sensations against the core. Elven juices and sweat clung to the orb's surface with each graze, matching the elf's loins in slimy defilement.

Flesh and goo quaked in unison as their bodies boiled from within. Liquids sprayed from the slime's surface as goosebumps once again covered Janara's arching form. A fever blanketed the elf's senses, and everything around her grew faint and dark.

Everything aside from what mattered.

Caresses, pulses, and shivers. She felt them so perfectly as a familiar energy swirled in her. Gathered in her. Seared in her. Until...

"Aaaaaaaaagh!" Their cries wove together down to the last echo as Eryss's form tickled every part of her. The fluids beneath the elf thinned, and Janara splashed into the moss.

The slime's membrane traded contractions with the elf's pussy as it embraced the elf to her bones, touching pleasurable parts that Janara didn't even know existed. A tensing elf leaked into a tensing slime who leaked into the earth. The shamefully inclined might have found this to be symbolic.

Janara's muscles relaxed as things were seemingly over, only for her cry to follow the membrane's clench one last time. It flattened her mound and rear as ooze coursed between her resting fingers.

There were two places her slime could've gone, and of course, it chose both. The elf's cry soon joined Eryss's as her congealed fluids pressured her holes.

Having both of her entrances taken was... interesting. It usually would have required two other people, but here she was, experiencing yet another luxury with just one talented elemental. It was a depraved thought and yet, that depravity swelled her with a thrill she had never felt before. A grimy thrill that only the filthiest of humans could've fantasized about and enjoyed.

And prude elves like her.

A stronger pulse roared through the slime, and it bored into her two separate innards for the first and second times. The heated bodies of liquid kneaded the thin wall between beginnings and ends. Pushing and pulling. Squeezing and rolling. Again and again.

Janara crossed her legs as her body contorted and her scream dominated the cave. For a second.

"Janar—Aaaah!" Eryss shrieked as a solid mass vibrated deep inside the elf's pussy. "My core! You're—Eeee! Take it out... please...!"

Sounds of not bliss, but of pain. The slime's pleas surged through the elf's nerves, demanding her muscles to act and choking her conscience with a long forgotten emotion.

A friend, a partner, a familiar in pain! She needed to... do something...

But it was so tiring, and so... dark...

And why wouldn't that terrible ringing noise go away...?

6

Reclamation

Enigmatic and infinite was sentience, so summoners knew not to fabricate it. Besides, there was no need given the abundance of complex life. The remains of any higher creature would do. All were suitable, from timeworn ashes to frozen husks.

That's what the Coven told her before assigning her here. The act itself was called *reclamation*, a nicer way of saying *gravedigging*, but that's what it basically was. More importantly, she was doing this as a favor to the deceased, and that notion spared her conscience.

It was long since she had snuck into the north, and longer since she could properly visit it. As a result, the crisp air was biting, even to her. Even with her heavy cloak. Even with all the manual labor.

Still, she had pressed on, and now her preparations were complete.

She tilted her head back to admire the snowflakes glittering against the gray sky. The walls of the narrow chasm glistened with water, and the ambient light cast a deep blue hue in the area. The depth of the frozen lake was unmatched, and only the blessing of an earthen tremor could've granted her this opportunity.

There it was, the frozen husk in front of her. So the Coven spoke the truth, after all.

Only a particular kind of soul would do. Those who passed from age had reason but no will, while beasts had will but no reason.

What good was it to have a familiar who didn't want to be alive? Those who commanded from fear risked untimely ends from summons who forced their return to paradise. The Coven had a name for that too: conjurcide.

Her nails clicked across the corpse's noose and heart-bound arrow before she tested the ropes on the corpse's legs and the connected rocks beneath.

The humans really wanted this person dead.

A flick of her fingers warped the body and its trinkets to the splattered circle, and another flick floated her codex onto a gap in the markings. She placed her freshly cut hand atop the tome's pages.

Fo hrl sglmheg'i nbb, fnjd hrni iepb he anjl. An unknown voice whispered in her mind as she tore her hand from the tome.

The timing was rather strict. Too little of that voice and the ritual wouldn't finish, whereas too much would have driven her mad. Good thing she'd practiced over one hundred times.

As the glowing circle's runes settled onto the body's fractured surface, a soft hum filled the air before they dissipated. Lightning echoed from the sky onto the body, overwhelming her eyes with white as flakes of ice and water drizzled onto her.

The air was sweet and pungent as the noose and arrows burned until only dust remained, and the tied stones and the husk followed soon after. Only a pile of white powder stood within the circle now.

After dismissing her book, she retreated a few paces up the sloped path. Water crashed against the frozen sides of the rift before settling into a small pond. There, the ashes churned and swirled.

No... Leave her out of this...! Fragments of a feminine voice skimmed her mind.

The ashes dissolved into the water and it thickened, grew, and molded into the shape of a woman roughly the same height as her. Light splintered as it hit the slime's figure, covering the ice cave in rainbow flecks, and bubbles pierced her mouth as she gasped for air. Amusingly, they traveled through her head before popping at the top.

"I'm... alive?" gurgled the slime.

"How do you like it?"

The slime's movements were as slow as the surrounding slush. She peered at a flat hunk of ice before turning her attention to her translucent hands. Her face scrunched up and a terrible noise shuddered the summoner's ears.

Drip drop. Drip drop. The walls preserved that sound for what seemed like forever.

They had sentenced the former human to death for witchery. Surely that was someone who would have wanted a second chance at life. Or did the Coven lie? Did she wrong them in a way that warranted death? Some simple feedback would have worked, too.

"Hey!" Water stained the summoner's cloak as she stumbled through the shallows toward the slime. Within her clothes, she unsheathed a runed dagger and eyed the creature's core. "Don't cry, I can reverse the—"

She gritted her teeth as two rimed arms wrapped around her. The chill pierced through her clothes and into her flesh. A wise person would have recoiled back, perhaps with enough force to tear the elemental's arms right off.

So, of course, she did not.

"Thank you...!" The slime's voice was breathless and strained as she pressed her body into the cloak's opening, drenching the front of the summoner's clothes. "I thought it'd be dark and cold forever..."

Clang! A powerful shiver freed the knife, and both turned to it with widened eyes.

The slime tensed and lurched backward until her back flattened against the ice. "What were you planning with that knife?!"

"Self-defense." The summoner picked up the dagger and sighed. "You seemed distressed."

"Oh..." The slime drifted back to her and ran her hand across the knife. "It looks different." She shuddered. "How long has it been?"

"It's the tenth age. Third year, third month, first day, to be exact."

"Tenth?!" Her fingers attempted to scratch her head, only to pass through it. "And my village?"

She resheathed the dagger. "If time didn't claim it, the war probably did. I'm sorry."

"Ah... so all those people..." The elemental's eyes dissolved while her nucleus fluttered within her body. Time passed, and a chuckle grazed the silence as her eyes reformed. "I'm grateful to not share their fate."

She extended a hand to the slime and grinned. "Then the Coven and I welcome you to our ranks!"

Maybe it was a more appropriate gesture to someone more solid, but it felt right as their trembling hands met as best they could.

"Let's depart." The summoner pointed at the ascending trail. "There's no telling when the ice will collapse."

After a shiver and a nod, the slime followed.

Long was the hike out of the lake, but longer was the summoner's story to the slime. Great wars, societal collapse, revolutions, and everything else. It felt weird telling the former human of the horrors her successors had bequeathed the world, but the slime regretfully understood and accepted her new loyalties.

Humans weren't all bad. The Coven had some good ones if one considered *good* to mean *not genocidal*, and the best of those wished for a world where they all got along. Of course, those were just words, and were an easy thing to say when one's kind controlled more than half the continent.

The world brightened as the pair reached the surface and then her camp. Not a cloud painted the sky as the sun beamed down, and the air was warm and inviting.

Fog had limited her gaze of the surroundings on her ingress to the lake, but now she could see far into the distance. A jagged mountain range guarded the far north, while evergreens fuzzed the horizon in all other directions, and shades of black and white grained the landscape.

If she had more time, supplies, and fortitude, all she had to do was cross that northern ridge, and she'd be... uhh, in Frostian territory. The guards would probably let her in by appearance alone, and she'd once again enter her native lands. That place seemed to change each time she visited, so she always needed a break afterward to process everything.

She spread her cloak over the thawed grass before sitting down, and a flick of her fingers sparked the darkened logs.

The slime watched the flame from the opposite side, perhaps to avoid wetting the summoner's clothes again. She eyed the ragged bedroll, the fire, and the lack of anything else. "Umm, not to be rude, but your dwelling seems a bit bare."

"This was just for retrieving you. We're going south, through the human lands, to get home." She yawned before pulling her legs to her chest and bringing her hands toward the fire. "But we've a long way to go, so let's rest first."

The slime reached toward it too, and she sighed as the frost on her arms thawed.

They grew drowsy despite their grins in the sunshine, but that was to be expected. One hadn't slept for what seemed like ages, and the other hadn't slept for actual ages. The flame's cozy veil only added to the exhaustion.

"I hope we'll be great friends, Janara..."

7

Witnesses

Sandy howls twitched her ears as the black withered away.

Janara ran a hand from her neck to her abdomen. It was cool and strangely dry, like the flora beneath her. After rubbing her temples, the green and gray blurs in her vision overlapped into clarity.

Eryss remained still, keeping her back to the elf as she stared across the emptied pool.

Memories spilled into Janara, sending a shiver down her spine. A bad, terrible, well-deserved shiver. The slime had pled for mercy, and she failed to protect her. Janara had violated her oath as a summoner and as a friend.

She couldn't recall the last time they had fought. If Eryss had a temper, she had never experienced it, and that worsened the dread as Janara peered around the darkened cave, trying to delay the inevitable conversation.

Janara scratched her shoulders and gritted her teeth as she dragged herself to Eryss. The moss dulled her footsteps, but it'd hide little from someone who was partially fused to the vegetation. Every step grew squishier and squishier, offering a very obvious noise, and if that didn't alert the slime, the elf was pretty much walking on her, too.

As Janara closed the distance, the core in the slime's chest froze for a moment before resuming its swaying.

She cleared her throat and rolled an ear between her fingers. "H-hey, Eryss."

"You looked so peaceful asleep. I didn't want to wake you." The slime morphed to face her. "And I'm not hurt, but you did ruin my enjoyment at the end there."

"Sorry about that." The elf's ears drooped as she exhaled deeply.

"So..." A goofy smile grew on the slime's lips as she drifted closer to the elf. "Can we have a redo? I'd like to try something different, if you don't mind."

Oh Eryss, as resilient as the water that composed her. Janara should've known that a few squeezes wouldn't trouble her familiar. Especially after everything else the slime had endured.

"I'm all yours," said Janara.

"Just stay right there, my cute elf."

Eryss dove into the ground, intertwining with the moss as the vegetation pulsed beneath the elf's feet. Several distinct masses churned, gathered, and bubbled under Janara until they swelled upward to match her height.

Their bodies emerged from the splattering goo, slowly increasing in details. Now a group of Erysses surrounded the elf, and each bore a particular expression. Some looked excited, others looked scheming, and a few were somewhere in between.

"Never thought I'd have a harem." Janara chuckled.

The slime on her left asked, "Should I look like that dust elf instead?"

"His succubus?" asked the rightward slime.

Another voice came from behind. "Or maybe... an equal number of both?"

"Right now, I only want my best friend," said the elf.

The cored one in front of Janara nodded before moving closer, and the ring of coreless clones followed.

Being able to appreciate Eryss so closely and openly made the slime even more tempting. Better than that ungrateful succubus for sure, and there were so many to admire, too.

But the greatest thing of all was how they all shared the elf's feelings. She couldn't have asked for more from an entourage of her best friends. Just what did they have planned for her?

Four of the smiling slimes flowed closer to her. The one in front wrapped her arms around the elf, flattening their ample and modest breasts against each other and engulfing her torso perfectly. The slime behind also pushed into her, filling every lovely crease on her back as her sticky bosom spread apart.

Janara's breaths fogged the first Eryss's face as she gazed into her pupilless eyes. While her core rattled in her head, their grins built upon one another, becoming more and more ridiculous.

After flanking the elf, the two remaining slimes pinned Janara's arms between their breasts while grinding their featureless nethers against the elf's palms. Then their heads leaned forward until their lips touched her eartips, and the slimes nipped them a few times before swallowing the elf's dagger-ears to their bases.

As thousands of tiny tongues explored her ears' creases, the Eryss behind her alternated kisses and licks on her neck as her gooey hands slipped over the elf's pinned breasts.

There she fondled her, jiggling the dainty bumps as her nipples ran against the rear slime's fingers and the front slime's chest. It didn't take long for Janara's nubs to dimple Eryss's membrane.

For a former human, Eryss knew elven bodies well. Maybe humans liked to be touched and licked in those places, too. Or maybe, given how close her village was to that mountain range...

The elemental before her gave a comforting look before the flanking slimes popped off her ears. That was all it took for Janara to groan through her teeth and for her eyes to pinch shut.

"You're making that adorable face again!" The clones giggled in tandem as a fuzzy warmth surged through the elf's body. Janara never doubted her own beauty, but hearing about it from others was refreshing, especially after the succubus tried to tear her down.

It was equally adorable seeing Eryss break through her reserved nature. Living as a human and then as a slime required adaptations, both physically and mentally. She had gotten so much more confident since then, and today she had found enough enjoyment and poise in her new body to share it with her best friend.

And what a beautiful smile she had! Her lips had a brilliant gloss that adorned the rich fluids within. She needed to get a closer look...

The slimes jumped, and their laughter ceased. "Janara?!"

All their eyes were upon her now.

Something cool touched her lips, for her face had drawn close to the slime's on its own. Eryss's eyes were hypnotic as water trickled down her cheeks like sweat.

The elf bolted back as if she could still undo things, but a trail connected their mouths, refusing to tear, and there were plenty of witnesses.

Their gazes danced in and out of each other as their lips quivered. They had eaten each other out with little reservations, but a kiss was... special.

The elf coughed. "Just rehearsing! For Alsindor!"

Was it really for practice or did something rouse in her? The slime understood everything about Janara, and if Eryss was... err, if she wasn't, umm... then maybe... Everything was a mess right now, but the elf knew one thing for sure.

"If you wanted to kiss, all you had to do was ask," said the cored Eryss.

The grinning slime squished their faces back together as their eyes eased. The elf's jaw was loose and her gooey tongue slipped through the gaps in her teeth. There, she explored the elf's inner cheeks before snaring her tongue and abducting it into her translucent mouth.

The gel at Janara's feet raised her until her head tilted down to the slime. Plenty of drool passed from her lips to Eryss's as the slime's squishy mouth caressed her captive tongue.

"Such a delicious elf." The clone behind the elf pushed her head forward, flattening their kissing lips as Eryss sucked her tongue dry.

She lowered Janara back down and freed her tongue, leaving an earthy coating on it as they continued their embrace.

The slimes at her sides resumed suckling her ears while three more copies formed and joined the pile. Two of them wedged themselves against her chest, and each one dedicated herself to a nipple. Her nubs had eased despite Eryss's efforts, and the fresh sensation of the clones' slurps rehardened them instantly.

Her last copy sunk out of sight until a peck on her clit revealed her role. The copy's fingers dimpled Janara's rear as the other slimes offered their hands to her nethers. They spread the elf open, baring her pink insides for all to see. Janara shivered and dripped as the air cooled her folds, and again when the slime dug in.

The kneeling clone's tongue drilled through her depths and flooded her innards. Then it grew, filling up all of her until her walls could no longer squeeze back. Every so often the slime pulsed, and that sensation quaked through the elf, making her thighs clasp the copy's head.

The two duplicates at Janara's side spread her legs, opening her up further before another slime jammed herself between her thighs, partially fusing with the clone already present.

A few laps of their tongues turned the elf's legs into jelly, and the copies thickened to support her, suspending her into the air once more. Janara gripped the ooze at her sides, which promptly morphed into hands for her to hold.

Eryss definitely had a special someone in the past.

Then a new feeling loomed from within Janara. It was deep. Deeper than her fingers and deeper than where the slime's tongue had first gone.

The goo had been ebbing and flowing against the firm ring at the back of the elf's tunnel for quite some time, and now it had loosened from all the excitement. Eryss's presence tided in and out of the delicate channel connecting her sheath to her untouched cradle.

Some overshot her duct, ending up inside her womb and making her abs clench. As the entrenched goo vibrated, her cramps turned blissful, and her hands wrung plenty of liquid from the slimes' grasp.

Their mouths remained connected, and the elf's cries floated through Eryss's head, grazing her core on the ascent as she moaned back. Only when the bubbles burst above her gooey hair did Janara hear just how deafening she was.

Eryss drank in Janara's drool, sweat, and juices as the elf writhed atop the sinful mound of elementals. Despite the distracting pleasure, the core's motion stuck out to her, and she broke free from the slime's mesmerizing irises to track its descent. It passed through the membranes of several other slimes before teasing the elf's entrance.

So Eryss wanted to do that thing again. It was amazing how quickly she had changed her mind on it. By now, the gooey tides within her had receded, and the clones' attention was entirely on her nucleus, or rather, how to get it inside the elf.

The fist-sized core pressed against Janara's flesh, bringing forth pain and pleasure as the mass eased in, stretching her to her limits. While her entrance relaxed, her folds gripped the slime's organ for dear life as slime flooded in behind the orb, ready to submerge the nucleus within her.

Muscles and slime flushed the core into the elf's depths, and flesh grazed against flesh on its dive. Its rough surface hit all her spots perfectly once more, and as Janara drooled into Eryss's mouth, she drooled back a thicker fluid that persisted through several swallows. A similar liquid embedded itself within the elf, and by now her insides were as elven as they were gooey.

Finally, her organ nestled against her cervix, spurting more slime into her deepest part as her hole pulsed. Lightning shot through the elf, tensing her muscles as her walls mashed the orb. Her body wrapped the heavenly mass in its flesh and juices, demanding that it remain at that wondrous spot.

Eryss's heart, brain, nucleus, whatever—the part of her that could think, feel, and control her fluids—was inside the elf at that moment, buried deep within her like an extra organ she didn't know she needed. And Janara thought being hugged by all those Erysses at once was as close as she would get to her.

Ohhh... Janara couldn't describe the feeling in words.

Outside, the hands that had spread her open now caressed a bump in her abdomen. The elf's tunnel resonated as the core burrowed into the hard flesh at the end of her sheath. Janara could've sworn it was fusing to her cervix. Slime glued their organs together, guarding against any expulsions while the elf tensed.

Their heartbeats and temperatures matched, and the copies' moans harmonized with Janara's as they clenched as one. Eventually, those clenches diminished into stillness.

A jerk of their bodies made the elf send an enormous bubble through the slime's head, and its pop splattered goo everywhere.

"Aaaaaaaaaaaaaaaaaah!" The elf's voice echoed through the cave.

Janara's ears dipped as the core froze within her and the cavern went silent. Her heart beat quickly, not from bliss, but from something else. Something bad.

"I've adapted to it," said the slime in front.

"Focus on your own pleasure, and mine will follow," said the slime behind her.

Typical Eryss, always attentive to minute details. Then again, their chests had practically merged, and their heartbeats were so synchronized that any deviance would've been obvious, even to Janara.

The elf shut her eyes as she thought of more important things, like how depraved everything was right now.

An orgy of tongues feasted on her ears, nape, and pussy while countless eyes watched Janara act the lewdest she'd ever been. A powerfully ranked Covener, melting within a harem of slime girls. How scandalous!

The core's movements were visible even on the outside as it massaged her insides perfectly. Meanwhile, goo drenched every part of the elf's flesh—inside and out.

Externally, the ooze penetrated deep into the elf's pores as the clones' curves flattened against her figure. Arms, legs, faces, breasts, and everything else embraced her all at once in a writhing pile of body parts.

Gods, the sensation of their overlapped membranes against her skin was almost enough to make her come right there. They had clung to each other for so long that the goo felt like a part of her.

The elf's ears throbbed with delight as her abs flexed against the orb inside her. As the slimes' voices pitched higher with the elf's, their bodies grew rigid and shaky.

The Erysses cried out first, nearly crushing her as they solidified. Only the fluids around Janara's head stayed soft. Despite the pressure, it was strangely calming and felt good in a wholesome sort of way, like being hugged multiple times at once.

This must have been how Eryss felt inside her.

Heat coursed into the elf next, and Janara ruptured the slimes' hands as she tore her arms away. Her hands darted to the original Eryss's back, tracing its intricacies upward before clutching the slime's head. Then she pulled her close and their lips touched once more.

The swirl in the slime's eyes paused momentarily before resuming, and she, too, leaned into the elf. After shoving aside countless clones, Eryss pressed her front into Janara, and they joined like a mold and its creation.

With a slurp, the slime's sweet tongue thrust past the elf's lips. Parts of it broke off, joining with Janara's saliva as she swallowed, filling her throat and belly with an animated warmth.

Janara desired more, so her tongue raked across the slime's, wresting more of her amazing fluids. Then, desiring even more, Janara sucked her tongue, wringing a deluge from Eryss that was replaced as fast as the elf sipped.

Heaven buzzed within Janara, and her vision and the surrounding groans waltzed and smeared around her. This time, she knew her best friend would enjoy it, too.

It started as a clench as elven fluids trickled from every inner pore, managing a quick descent before its capture by the slime. Those rhythms strengthened, and soon her pussy trembled as it crushed and tore at the mass inside her.

Finally, the membrane within her burst and nectar seared down her legs for the goo beneath to absorb. An elven tang became increasingly apparent in Eryss's ooze, and Janara sucked harder on the slime's tongue, loving how they tasted together.

Their scents mingled, steaming into the air as the slime's surface boiled. Janara's breaths were deep, not from exertion, but because she needed more of that honeyed taste and scent inside her.

By now, the elementals had crowded her again. Two on her ears, one each on her nape, mouth, and pussy, and plenty more that were unseen but felt. They thrashed the petite elf against their sticky bodies, and as the elf thrashed back, the slimes clumped together, becoming less distinct as they merged.

The passing storm couldn't even compete against their joined howls.

With a pop, their kiss broke and fragments of the slime's tongue stuck to the elf's teeth, disintegrating as it mingled with her saliva but remaining potent. Janara swallowed every drop.

Heat gushed out of her hole as something tumbled through her folds. Her abs squeezed until a plop sounded with another pleasured shudder and a stream of fever. Eryss's core tickled her inner thighs before it reentered the slime and floated back into her head, looking redder than usual.

The elf's world fogged and darkened at the edges, and their sounds muddied together so thoroughly she couldn't tell whose voice was whose. Janara's pinhole vision caught Eryss's delightful face and naughty grin, and she smirked in return.

As she settled into the pile of bodies, a pleasant darkness enveloped her.

8

Eternity

Janara roused to the cave's familiar ceiling with her back against the dry moss.

A pair of violet eyes greeted her as the two reached for each other, only for the elf's tiny hands to have little to grab onto as the slime's massive fingers slipped through the porous ground to snatch her up. They curled around the elf's body, offering a snug pressure that could've lulled her to sleep.

No slime clones remained, and it wasn't hard to guess where they had gone.

The slime hoisted Janara to eye level with her fingers clutching the elf beneath the arms like a doll. She peered down from the considerable height and clenched her thighs together.

What was this feeling?

Maybe it was Eryss's size. Giant eyes, towering breasts, thick hips, and all the other hills and valleys. Janara thought she had enjoyed them to their fullest extent before, but now there was just so much more to appreciate.

Or maybe it was the tenderness. Eryss's hold was gentle as she stroked the elf's hair with a finger, and the thought of such a powerful monster treating her like this was soothing.

Yep, it was definitely both, and that slummy city's slummy residence could wait. If she didn't have to worry about food or curfews, she would have stayed in the cave, sleeping within Eryss's comforting embrace.

Her lips looked beautifully full as the giant hand brought Janara closer. The orgy with the clones was fresh in her mind, as was the texture of her exquisite core, so what outlandish things did Eryss have planned for her now?

She answered the elf's thoughts with a lick of her lips and a noisy swallow that flushed goo from her throat to her jiggling belly. The giantess lifted her morsel higher as she opened her translucent mouth. There were so many details there too! She must've thoroughly explored the elf's mouth back then.

"Such a delicious elf..." Eryss's voice quaked the cavern.

Janara wasn't even inside her yet, but she could already feel it. Fluids swirled everywhere in the toothless, throatless cavity, ready to tease every part of her. As the hand brought her closer, the elf tugged an ear and gulped.

That tongue of hers looked especially soft and sweet, and its smaller form felt so good against her skin and insides back then. Now it was as big as she was, and coming closer.

First, it was her desire. While the succubus cracked that closet's door, Eryss blew it open. Now, it was her decency as she dripped from the thought of being eaten by such a powerfully pretty slime.

Even though she was safe, her pulse quickened at the thought of what could have been. A different slime, a different personality, and she'd be dinner right now.

Eryss's tongue snagged a foot and the chill tensed Janara's body as the organ dragged Janara onto her lips. As strings of goo frayed off the elf's back, the slime sucked on her leg, dragging her body into the slime's mouth until just her head peeked out. Her nipples grazed against Eryss's squeaky lips as her tongue flipped the elf over.

Now she stared at the slime's bouncy rack.

Animated saliva slithered across her face, and now not a part of her escaped the touch of her gel. She could only watch through the glassy skin as that hulking tongue wrangled her body. It smacked her chest, pinning her lower half to the mouth's top while it spilled to her sides. Her skin stretched as it tried to squirm against the tongue's suction, and the elf remained where she needed to be.

The difference in size made the tongue's bumpy texture and pulses so much more apparent as they traced the elf from her abs to her neck. It was as if hundreds of fingers were feeling her up all at once.

With the elf captured, Eryss hummed as she worked the tongue between the elf's thighs. Janara's arms and legs hugged the organ as the jelly vibrated over her folds. Her limbs squeezed the tongue, strangling liquids from it like a wet towel as a strange mix of moans and laughter left her lungs.

The goo crept across her delicate muscles like a second skin, moving in cadence with the slime's song as her tongue worked itself into her folds, where it continued to purr. The elf's heat diffused into the engulfing fluids, which returned it tenfold, swaddling her already fevered body.

She humped against the tongue as she held on as best she could, and the finger-sized tastebuds skittered past her clit over and over, making ecstasy trickle from her entrance.

Squeak, squeak, squeak. Her grunts followed those ear-shivering sounds, gaining as their fluids smudged each other.

A rough thrust peaked her body, summiting her cries while her limbs hollowed the tongue against her. Elven juices trailed the tongue's underside as its lumps burrowed into the elf's folds and thrashed her nub.

Another rough thrust, another cry, and Janara collapsed as she peaked again. Her ears firmed and pulsed while her hips rolled, flattening the tongue's studs against her body as they embraced deeper and deeper. Its tip teased her neck and chin, lapping away her drool as the muscles tensed there.

Janara's eyes rolled back as far as they could while her body laid limp in the slime's mouth, the prey having succumbed to the predator. Every aftershock contracted her tunnel and offered more fluids to be assimilated by the slime.

After the tongue slowed and life returned to her, Janara held its tip to her lips and kissed deeply, sucking in part of it as she inhaled the addictive, dizzying musk. A deeper draw soothed her parched throat as the membrane surrendered some of its inner fluids.

Janara freed the tongue from her embrace, and it gifted her a last lick as the elf's fluids trickled from the tongue to the back of the dominating mouth.

As the elf's surroundings cooled, her heart and eyes slacked with a frost that shuddered her, but not from its bite. It reminded her of that frozen lake from her erstwhile homeland.

She'd been searching for something... anything, since that day. Any memento to prove that those lands weren't just a dream conjured by her mind to stay sane. When the need for remembrance had finally pierced through her escapist fantasies, all those pendants and trinkets were lost.

But all along, Eryss was...

Janara gave the tongue another peck as something warmer than sweat trickled down her cheek.

Not a peep sounded from the elf as the giant lips opened around her. The tongue caught her fall with a splash and she slid into a featureless dead end where the slime's throat would've begun.

The slime's tongue crushed her against the back of the mouth, stretching the membrane until the elf slipped inside. Goosebumps formed across Janara's body as warm fluid crawled across its curves and creases.

When the last part of her became engulfed, Eryss's insides became her world. Her hums rang into the elf's ears, her taste burrowed into the elf's tongue, and her goo suffocated her vision.

After a brief descent, her body rebounded upward some distance as the current collapsed on her. The deluge of liquid forced out a breath, and Janara watched while its blue-tinged blur fluttered out of reach. Blood rushed within the elf and her limbs thrashed, grasping for support and getting nothing as the goo absorbed her motions.

"I oxygenated myself. Breathe it in..." said a muffled voice outside.

Ah yes, the protective feeling that had made Janara throw herself at the mercy of the giant slime in the first place. Here's where it came in. But drowning to not drown... If only it were that easy to convince her ignorant body to do such a thing.

Could water elementals synthesize oxygen? Did it come from the air or their water content? The carbon dioxide would also have to come out too, right? Could lungs even extract oxygen from a liquid? Water, no, but what about a water elemental's essence...?

Her airway refused to budge, and a different foggy feeling returned. The bad kind.

Focus, she needed to focus. The frozen lake, the trek back to the hideout, and all those adventures thereafter. What was Janara so worked up about? Eryss had spent the same restless nights as she did studying slimes. And she was one, damn it!

Military Applications of Hydroplasm familiaris, chapter thirty-four, section six. Yes, that was the one. Janara's heart calmed as she surrendered to the slime.

Eryss's squeeze slipped air from her mouth and nostrils, and goo rushed in to fill the void. It tickled her vocal cords as more bubbles left her through a silent cough. Another bubbly cough, another one, and then another one. Less and less came out and more and more came in with each choke until the exchange left her emptied.

Her chest felt heavy and tingly, and the elf would've fallen over had the slime not thickened around her. Janara made an empty gasp as the ooze slipped down the other pipe as well.

In any other scenario, she would've retched, but Eryss's fluid matched Janara's temperature so perfectly. Its weight was the only reminder of its presence in her as it streamed into her numbing lungs and stomach, swelling her chest and belly slightly.

Fog and fear faded from the elf as the slime embraced her on the inside and outside. One clench spread the coziness through her flesh, and another clench leeched it into her bones.

What senses did she even have left? Light and sound muffled at this depth and the oversaturation numbed her nose and tongue.

Fluids teased her limbs and lips as she stretched and yawned. Maybe it'd be okay sleeping in the cave—in Eryss—just this once. Her record was mostly spotless, and the sandstorm offered a perfect excuse for her tardiness.

Besides, she had a water elemental to enjoy right now.

Janara felt it all while she floated inside Eryss like a rag doll, as if she were part of the slime. The swaying of her membrane, the ebb and flow of her ooze, and the muted pulses of her core... somewhere.

Were her eyes opened or closed? Things looked the same either way.

The liquid rolled across the elf, and she shivered against its density. They were teasing touches, and Janara bore no resistance as Eryss explored her. The elf's heavy breaths merely whirled the ooze within her as her lungs refused to empty.

Eryss grew bolder, and the fluid descended upon her body, brushing across her clit and holes. Janara's arms and legs spread apart as the sensation built, and the elf's spine shimmied as the slime's fluids trickled into both entrances, clinging to and climbing her insides.

The goo brushed against her cervix, thumping the elf's heart as Eryss nudged and then prodded it. A wave gathered at her entrance before it crashed into the ring of muscle, and the elf contorted as goo seeped into her womb. Until today, nothing had ever touched her so deeply before, and while it filled her to the brim, every little movement sloshed it within her.

Janara clutched her belly, enjoying the slight bump and softer texture that had replaced her firm abs. Every poke and jostle of her fingers scratched a primal urge deep within her she never knew existed.

The trickles increased to a surge as the flood claimed the last recesses of her body. Slime suffused her intestines and pussy, adding to the stomach's swell on her rumbling belly. Ooze expanded and contracted within the elf's womb, pussy, and rear, making her lower half convulse as she saw stars.

Stars that blurred as Eryss hummed again. Through the blinding goo, Janara could barely make out two violet circles gazing down at her. Pervert.

Goo swabbed her eardrums on every pulse, and her ears slowly fluttered in the thick ooze as a shivering feeling returned to their tips. The ooze between her clit and hood buzzed, and its effects inside her holes were just as strong.

Smart slime. No need to find a woman's melting points if one serviced everything equally.

Fluids churned around her, some of which were certainly hers. It never ascended beyond a mild whirlpool, but that was all Eryss needed to captivate the elf.

It trickled in and out of her cervix, sloshed against her womb walls, swirled around her clit, and it stuffed her pussy and rear. They were ordinary events on their own, but c-combined they were...

Janara swelled her lungs with fluid and held it in. What a dangerous slime, eating up such an innocent elf. She shut her eyes tight as she imagined how Eryss felt at that moment.

The feeling of having prey trapped within... Eroding said prey via an endless drip-feed of bliss... Feasting on every one of their subtleties and d-desires... All while her presence made its way into every one of her victim's pores... d-drilling deep as it...

So would J-Janara become part of her as well? F-f-fused with her core? Or... or—

Aaaaaaaaaaaaaa... That sound radiated in her mind for what seemed like forever, and her vocal cords gurgled silently as it tried to copy.

Her mind... her body... everything was melting... There had to have been enzymes, drugs, pheromones, or something in the goo... How could mere water bring her to her knees like this?!

From the tips of her ears, the heat trickled down her body in a bubbling tide before flushing out her holes. No flails, no screams, and no... anything really came from the conquered elf. Bliss gathered atop an existing bliss as Eryss worked the stilled elf through the afterglow like a puppet.

The water reversed direction, and the feeling retreated up her body, escaping through a choked gasp as a tiny bubble. Then the flow rocked back and forth, up and down, and side by side as her body boiled in pleasure. Eryss randomized the direction, so every shift brought the elf to a shiver as it grazed an unexpected part of her.

It didn't take long for Janara to come again. Over and over and over and over, she tided and receded through the various phases of rapture. As every facet infused her at once, the lines between foreglow, excursion, edge, orgasm, and afterglow blurred into an eternal paradise.

Was Eryss's core always in front of her, and when did it become so big? Janara embraced the slime's heart, sinking into its folds as it sucked her in. The brilliant violet of her flesh crawled over the elf's vision as Eryss's insides devoured her whole, and soon all she could hear were the slime's heartbeats. Every pulse echoed through her being as if they were one.

The nucleus engulfed every crease and curve of hers as she curled into a ball. It gently rocked, perhaps to distract her from the fleshy hairs that prodded, twisted, and wormed against her. Once again, their temperatures matched, and Janara couldn't tell where her flesh ended and Eryss's began.

Aside from her thoughts, she couldn't really feel anything anymore. Not being able to move turned into wondering whether she even had limbs or a body, and everything looked, tasted, smelled, sounded, and felt like nothing. Then came a swaddling darkness that nipped at the last piece of her consciousness.

If she drifted off at that moment, would she ever wake up again? Did it matter if she didn't wake up?

It wouldn't be so bad being part of Eryss. Yes, Eryss. That was her name now. A world without tears or stress or bills to pay, and where all her needs were met. With her best friend... *As* her best friend...

The scuffle in the library was so meaningless in the grand scheme of things, as was everything else she had done in her life.

"Umm... you know I'm not going to eat you, right?" Eryss loosened her nucleus's embrace, and light trickled in between the gaps.

"Of course you're not eating me. I have an assignment tomorrow!" Janara's hand shielded her eyes as the other pulled at the core's folds, demanding they close once more. "Can't a woman enjoy her fantasies once in a while?"

And so the dream continued.

9

Return

A cart had taken Janara the rest of the way to the desert capital. Bless those nocturnal centaurs.

The dawn's amber dripped down onto Stygia from a fracture miles above, painting silhouettes everywhere in the city. Usually, the place teemed with life—not a good sign for her timeliness.

"Halt! Elf, identify yourself!" The voice rallied through the barren streets.

Janara dripped sand and water as she jumped, and her feet rattled the road as she turned, face to face with...

Nothing.

A sniff from the guard dragged her eyes down to a pair of fluffy ears, matching the light brown of the short hair they protruded from. They laid flat for a moment before snapping to attention.

"Excuse me, my eyes are down here..."

Glasses adorned his humanoid face, both rounded, and a bushy tail flicked back and forth behind him. His hand shivered atop a sheathed knife at his side, and an insignia adorned his quilted armor.

Maple. Envoy of the city's dominant guild, and apparently also a night-shifting guard. There must've been a staffing shortage tonight.

"Five-thirteen." Her whisper may as well have been a shout.

He withdrew a book from a pouch on his back and flipped through the pages. The guard frowned, first at the tome and then at her. "Janara. You are ten hours past curfew. What is your explanation?"

"The sandstorm. I had to wait it out."

"That ended six hours ago."

"I... overslept. You know, lazy elves." Janara weakly shrugged.

His eyes tensed as he sniffed the air for a moment. Winds murmured from above as his eyes darted back and forth between the book and the elf.

Eventually, he sighed, and his expression relaxed.

"I'll overlook it this time." His hand left his weapon, and he smiled. "You are free to go."

Janara nodded, and Maple vanished as fast as he appeared.

Clack, clack, clack. The elf's footsteps prevailed once again as her assigned housing came into view.

The building was loud, cramped, smelly, hot, and plenty of other things one might've expected from a collective residence, and Janara only had a crate and bed she could've truly called her own. But where else could she properly rest with both of her eyes closed and her weapons forgotten? Elven organs fetched a hefty price in the human lands, encouraging hunters to prowl far and wide.

Not the north, not the heartland, and not even most of the Dustian Province. There was no place like home, and as meager as this place was, just being here was enough for her to forget about the day's worries, and plenty of Stygians would've sold their souls for what she had here.

After creeping through the snoring rows, Janara found her marked bed and crawled under its covers. Its excessive creaks and lumpy padding meant little to her as she drifted to black with a grin.

A new day, opportunity, and elf awaited her.

About the Author

I write erotic fantasy stories featuring monster girls.

Enjoy reading about voracious succubus tails, slime-girl clone harems, fluffy harpy wings, and much, much more. Nothing excites me more than exotic body parts and fantastical abilities being used in naughty ways, especially when there's an assertive monster girl taking charge.

Follow me on these platforms:

Website | cithrel.com
Newsletter | cithrel.com/newsletter
Twitter | twitter.com/cithrel
Goodreads | goodreads.com/cithrel

Join the Newsletter

Join my mailing list to stay updated with what I'm working on: cithrel.com/newsletter

As thanks for signing up, you'll also receive **a free digital copy of *Succubus With Benefits 1.5***, a book that isn't available anywhere else!

The story takes place right after the events of the first book. It features sensual bathing, a hands-on investigation into succubus anatomy, and a very lewd cover illustration.

Also by Cithrel

If you enjoyed the story, consider leaving a review and exploring another monstrous tale. Your support is always appreciated!

A very experienced succubus seduces her very innocent summoner.

A newsletter-exclusive freebie! The day after, a succubus helps her master come to terms with his new desires.

A harpy unwinds with the help of her two fluffy servants.

Printed in Great Britain
by Amazon

36992568R00046